The adventures of Charlotte and Henry

Bob Graham

Viking Kestrel

Contents

The Tire

The Tire

1. This is Henry.
   Henry worries a lot.

2. He worries
   about everything.

3. He worries
   about his dog,
   his parents...

4. and especially,
   most especially, he
   worries about his
   friend Charlotte.

5. Charlotte is wild
   and she does
   dangerous things.

6. Henry warns Charlotte, "Watch out, there's water in there."

7. Splash!

8. Henry and Charlotte push the tire to the top of the hill.

9. Henry calls, "Careful of the flowers!"

10. Charlotte jumps all around the tire —inside, outside, inside, outside—

11. and she runs all around the rim.

12. Uh, oh—the flowers!

13. "Watch me, Henry, I'm going to roll right down to the bottom of the hill."

14. "But Charlotte, it's too steep. It's dangerous.

15. "You'll go too fast and you'll land right in the bushes."

16. Charlotte says, "Oh, Henry, you're such a worrier."

8

17. Henry runs down
the hill as fast as
he can.

18. Charlotte crashes right through the bushes.

19. There is total silence.

20. The world is spinning round and round.

21. "Are you okay, Charlotte?"

"Of course I'm not. I've hurt myself!"

22. "Wait a minute. I'll rip up my shirt and make a bandage."

"Oh, Henry, don't do that."

23. "There, you're all set."

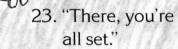

24. "You're nice, Henry. Do you know why?"

25. "Because you worry about everything…

26. "but then when I hurt myself, you don't say, 'I told you so.'

27. "But what's your mother going to say about your shirt?"

28. "Don't worry about it, Charlotte. It doesn't matter."

The Skipping Rope

The Skipping Rope

1. Henry is watching Charlotte skipping.

2. While she is skipping, she sings a song…

3. "Little Miss Pink

4. "fell down the sink.

5. "How many bubbles did she drink?

6. "One, two, three…" Henry is worried.

7. "Four, five, six…" Charlotte can skip to one hundred.

8. But not today.

9. Oops, her glasses!

10. Oof! Henry saves the day!

11. Without her glasses, Charlotte can't see very well.

12. Without her glasses, Charlotte sees three Henrys.

13. Henry has an idea.

14. He ties her glasses on with a piece of elastic.

15. Now the glasses stay on tight.

16. Charlotte can hang upside down…

17. she can shake her head…

18. she can do a
    somersault…

19. and her glasses
    don't fall off.

20. Charlotte brings
    her long skipping
    rope.

21. She ties one end
    to a tree

22. and gives the other end to Henry.
    "Go on, turn!"

23. Henry turns the rope.

24. Charlotte tries to skip.

25. But she has to skip all stooped over,

26. because whenever she stands up straight,

27. the rope hits her right on the glasses.

28. "Turn it *higher*, Henry." "I can't. My arms are too short."

29. Charlotte has an idea.

30. She makes Henry stand on a crate.

31. And that works just fine.

32. Now it's Henry's turn. Charlotte doesn't need the crate.

33. And her glasses stay on tight!

The Dolls

1. Charlotte is bored.

2. She tries listening to her radio

3. and putting on her mother's lipstick

4. and walking on her hands.

5. But she's still bored.

6. Charlotte goes to
   see Henry.

7. Henry is worried.
   He's very worried

8. because his dog
   Derby is losing
   his stuffing.

9. "How can you
   sleep with all that
   stuff on your bed,
   Henry?

10. "Who *are* they all,
    anyway?"
    "Be careful, Charlotte!

11. "That's Tess
    and Natalie
    and Petey
    and Little Pig,

12. "and that's Jasper, Humpty, Herbert, and the Mad Toucan,

13. "and, of course, Tirra Lirra Rabbit. He's missing an ear.

14. "And this one is Derby. He's my dog.

15. "And my bed is their home."
"Say, Henry, let's take them for a walk."
"No, they're fine right here."

16. "Here, Henry, just pass the string through·here…

17. "and I'll
tie this end
to the window…

18. "and throw this
end out on the
grass.

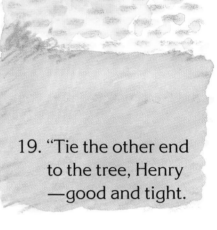

19. "Tie the other end
to the tree, Henry
—good and tight.

20. "Okay, now, all
aboard!"

21. "No, Charlotte! Don't!"
But down they go.

22. The basket goes faster and faster. It's going to hit the tree!

23. The basket hits the ground. Bump! The ride is over.

24. The basket turns gently on its side,

25. and Tirra Lirra Rabbit lands on his one remaining ear.

26. Poor Rabbit!

27. Henry rescues his friends.

28. Charlotte isn't bored any longer.

29. She gathers all the hangers.

30. "Here you go!

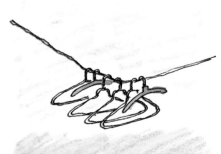

31. "You, too. And you, and you, and you…

32. "You're going to catch cold, Henry. Here comes your coat."

The Present

The Present

1. Henry is heartbroken.

2. His dog Derby has lost all his stuffing.

3. His family of friends just won't be the same. Charlotte thinks Henry's toys are silly

4. except when she makes up wild games for them.

5. Still, Charlotte doesn't like to see Henry so sad.

6. Charlotte has an idea. She will buy Henry a new Derby.

7. It will be a surprise. It will be a present.

8. Charlotte takes Derby when Henry's not looking. This way she can find a perfect match.

9. Now Henry is sadder than ever.

10. "Charlotte, I can't find Derby anywhere."
"Keep looking, Henry. He'll turn up."

11. But Charlotte has hidden Derby under her sweater.

12. She goes with her mother to all the toy shops.

13. But none of the animals look like Derby.

14. "No, Madam, we don't carry *this* model."

15. "Certainly not in *this* shop."

16. Charlotte finds some very nice penguins

17. and a huge brown bear riding a donkey

18. and some skates which she would like herself.

19. But she says, "The present is for Henry."

20. Charlotte has another idea. "Let's go home."

21. Charlotte cuts up some old tights and stuffs the pieces into Derby.

22. She finds a piece of material

23. and sews it onto Derby with some crazy stitches.

24. Perfect. It's all done.

25. Henry is delighted.

26. "You tricked me. You had Derby all the time."

27. "Do you like your new Derby dog, Henry?"
"I love him. Thank you, Charlotte."

28. "He's all fat and fuzzy again."

29. "And I can pretend that the patch is a saddle."

30. "But Henry, you don't put saddles on dogs."

31. "Can I roll him down the hill?"
"Oh no, Charlotte, not today."

The Dancer

The Dancer

1. Charlotte is taking dancing lessons.

2. She is doing her exercises in the bathroom.

3. She can see herself in the mirror,

4. but only her head

5. or her feet.

6. Charlotte has yellow legwarmers

7. and a black leotard.

8. She frightens Kim the dog.

9. Henry is not frightened,

10. but he is worried: Charlotte might break something.

11. Charlotte is a bit clumsy.

12. In the kitchen,
    she gets ready for
    her grand jeté.

13. She starts to run…
    Henry cries, "No, Charlotte, don't!"

14. Charlotte flies
    through the air.

15. Kim flies, too.

16. Charlotte and
    Kim fall…

17. Boom! What a landing!
    Kim thinks it's a fine game.

18. He wants to keep
    playing.

19. The cupboard is still shaking. Look out for the cup!

20. Good catch, Henry!

21. "Kim, get away from me."

22. "I know I can do a grand jeté, Henry."

23. "That's enough for today, Charlotte."

24. "Make Kim go
    away, Henry."

25. Bravo, Charlotte!

VIKING KESTREL
Viking Penguin Inc., 40 West 23rd Street, New York, New York 10010, U.S.A.
Penguin Books Ltd, Harmondsworth, Middlesex, England
Penguin Books Australia Ltd, Ringwood, Victoria, Australia
Penguin Books Canada Limited, 2801 John Street, Markham, Ontario, Canada L3R 1B4
Penguin Books (N.Z.) Ltd, 182–190 Wairau Road, Auckland 10, New Zealand

First published in France in five issues of *Les Belles Histoires de Pomme d'Api*
First published in one volume in France as *Les Aventures de Charlotte et Henri*
by Editions du Centurion, 1987. Copyright © 1987 Editions du Centurion/Les Belles
Histoires de Pomme d'Api
This English-language edition first published in 1987 by Viking Penguin Inc.
Published simultaneously in Canada

Printed in France

1   2   3   4   5   90   89   88   87

Library of Congress Catalog Card Number: 86-40610
ISBN 0-670-81660-4

By the same author

Pete and Roland